Chameleon comedian

Russell Punter

Illustrated by David Semple

Chameleon has dreams
of becoming a star.

Frog's
Cabaret Cl

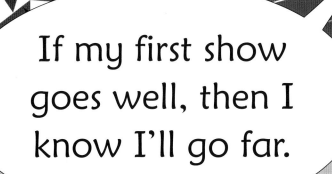

She waits by the stage,
and goes through her jokes.

Here's our last act tonight – meet Chameleon, folks!

But nobody laughs.

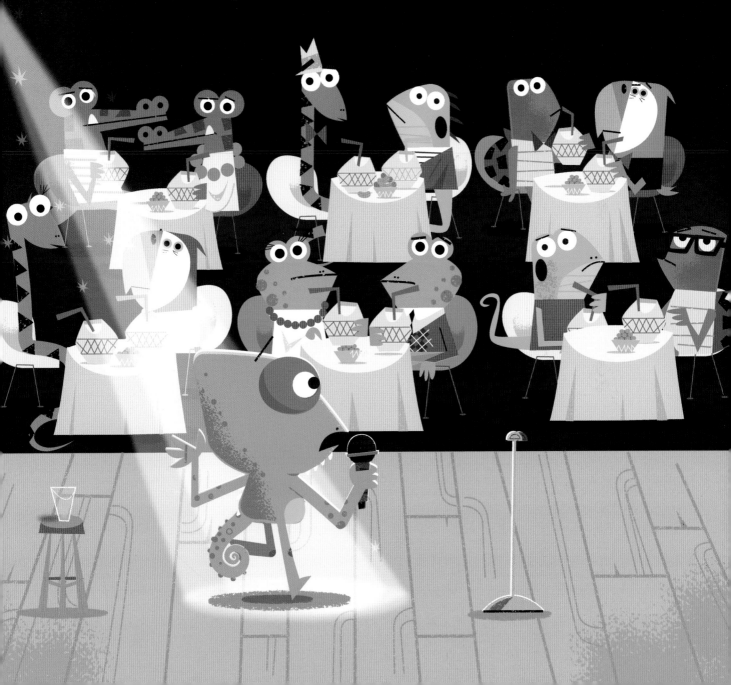

When Chameleon's uneasy
and can't seem to think...

her skin starts to turn
to a deep shade of pink.

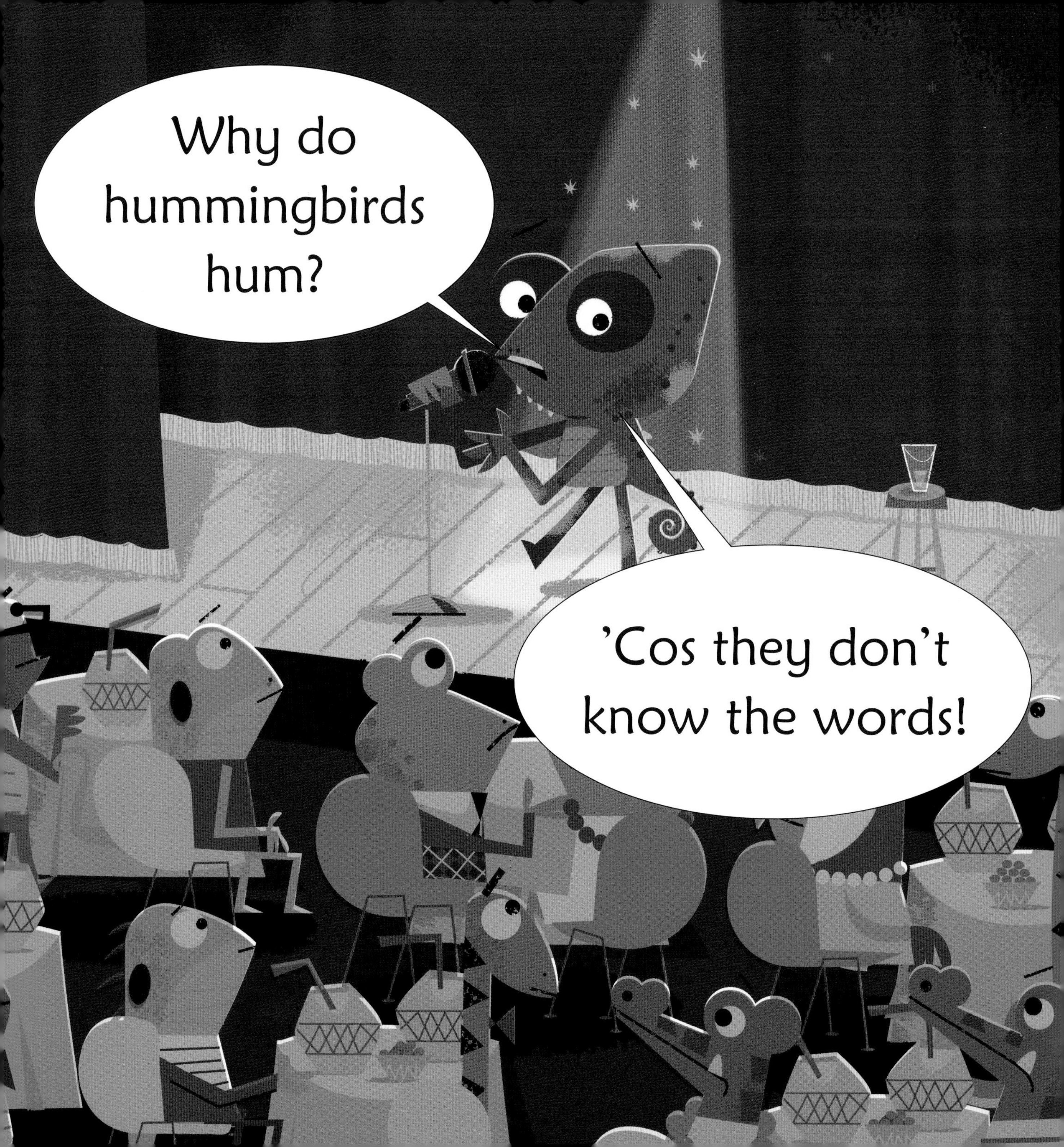
Why do hummingbirds hum?
'Cos they don't know the words!

There are grumbles and mumbles.

Not a chuckle is heard.

The crowd all walk out,
with loud shouts of "Boo!"

Now Chameleon's so red,
she has faded from view.

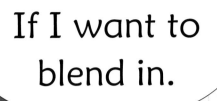

It's seven days later.
Chameleon's back.

But she's not
cracking jokes,
as she has a new act.

The Amazing
Chameleon

"I will enter this cabinet," Chameleon cries.

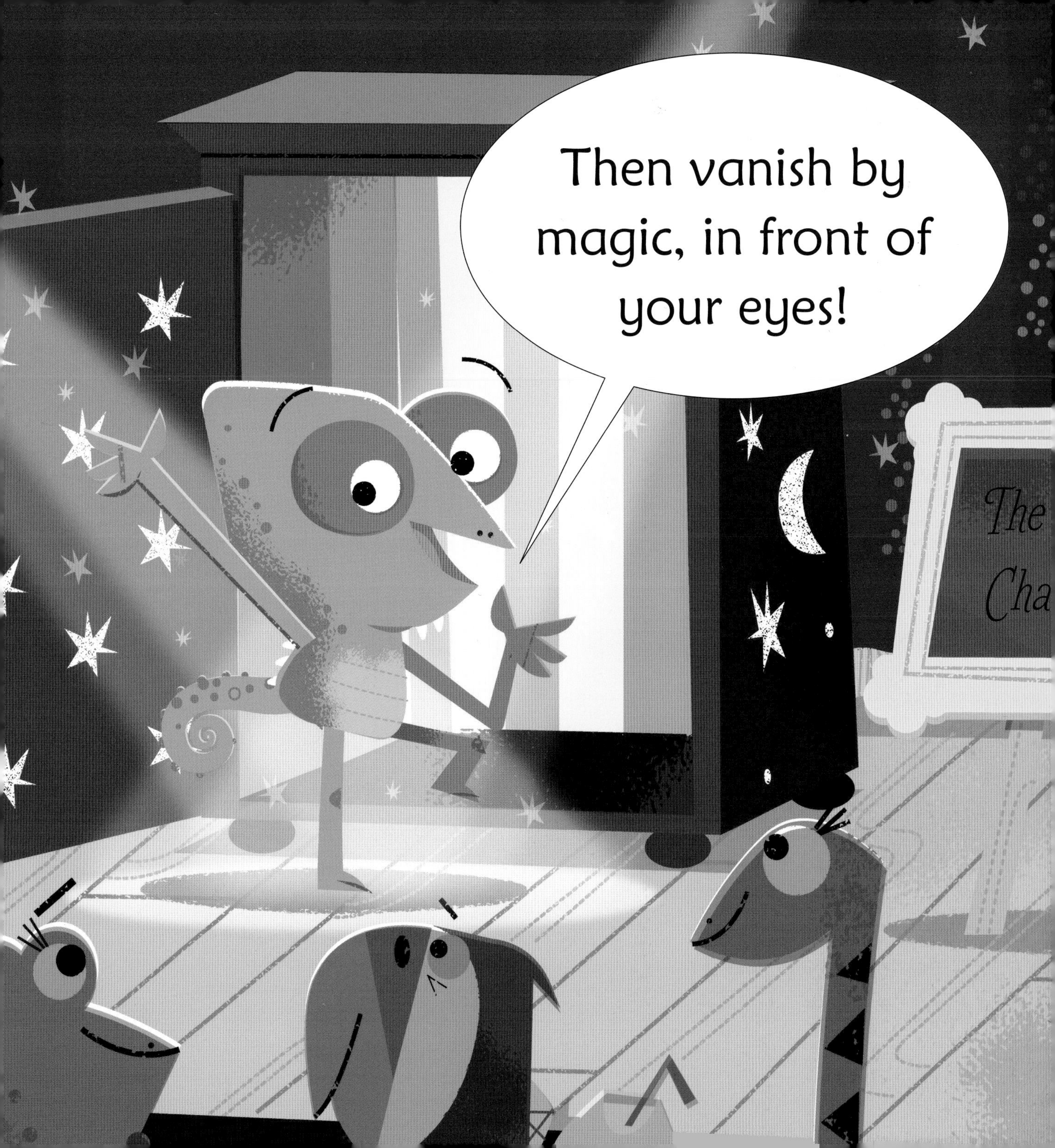
Then vanish by
magic, in front of
your eyes!

She climbs right inside,

then blends in. She's so slick.

Frog unlocks the door and...

About phonics

Phonics is a method of teaching reading which is used extensively in today's schools. At its heart is an emphasis on identifying the *sounds* of letters, or combinations of letters, that are then put together to make words. These sounds are known as phonemes.

Starting to read

Learning to read is an important milestone for any child. The process can begin well before children start to learn letters and put them together to read words. The sooner children can discover books and enjoy stories and language, the better they will be prepared for reading themselves, first with the help of an adult and then independently.

You can find out more about phonics on the Usborne Very First Reading website, **usborne.com/veryfirstreading** (US readers go to **veryfirstreading.com**). Click on the **Parents** tab at the top of the page, then scroll down and click on **About synthetic phonics.**

Phonemic awareness

An important early stage in pre-reading and early reading is developing phonemic awareness: that is, listening out for the sounds within words. Rhymes, rhyming stories and alliteration are excellent ways of encouraging phonemic awareness.

In this story, your child will soon identify the *e* sound, as in **chameleon** and **comedian.** Look out, too, for rhymes such as **jokes** – **folks** and **slick** – **trick**.

Hearing your child read

If your child is reading a story to you, don't rush to correct mistakes, but be ready to prompt or guide if he or she is struggling. Above all, do give plenty of praise and encouragement.

Edited by Jenny Tyler and Lesley Sims
Designed by Hope Reynolds

Reading consultants: Alison Kelly and Anne Washtell

First published in 2021 by Usborne Publishing Ltd., Usborne House, 83-85 Saffron Hill, London EC1N 8RT, England.
usborne.com Copyright © 2021 Usborne Publishing Ltd.